Weekly Reader Presents

Wembley
and the Soggy Map

By Louise Gikow · Pictures by Lisa McCue

Muppet Press
Henry Holt and Company
NEW YORK

Library of Congress Cataloging in Publication Data

Gikow, Louise.
Wembley and the soggy map.

Summary: When Wembley accidentally ruins Gobo's map,
he learns that being angry doesn't mean you stop caring
about someone.
[1. Anger—Fiction.   2. Friendship—Fiction.
3. Puppets—Fiction]   I. McCue, Lisa, ill.   II. Title.
PZ7.G369We   1986   [E]   85-18959

ISBN: 0-03-007242-5

Printed in the United States of America

ISBN 0-03-007242-5

"HEY, Gobo, what are you doing?" Wembley Fraggle bounced into the cave he shared with his best friend.

"I'm working on one of the maps my Uncle Traveling Matt left me," Gobo said, looking up. "See? I'm filling in some of these blank areas near the Crooked Caverns. Uncle Matt has never visited them."

"Nice map," Wembley said, leaning over Gobo's shoulder. "Do you want some of this radish shake? It's delicious."

"No thanks," Gobo said. "Hey! Be careful not to drip on the map! It's one of my best ones."

"I won't," Wembley said. "I promise!"

Gobo stood and stretched. "That does it for now," he said, smiling at his friend. "You know what I need? A nice, long walk. Want to come?"

"No thanks," said Wembley. "I think I'll just hang around here for a while."

"Okay, Wembley. See you!" Gobo waved as he walked out the door.

Wembley wandered around the cave for a little while, doing nothing in particular and feeling just fine. Then he went over to Gobo's desk to look at the map.

"Wow, Gobo must have worked really hard on it," he said to himself, leaning over to take a better look.

But as Wembley leaned over, his glass tilted. Before he knew what had happened, he had spilled the entire radish shake all over Gobo's map!

"Oh, no!" Wembley cried. "What did I do?" He looked at the map in horror, watching as the radish shake slowly seeped into the paper.

"I've got to clean it up!" Wembley put his glass down and started to run around in circles, looking for a rag. The only thing he could find was his other banana-tree shirt. He picked it up, ran back to the desk, and began gently blotting the map. But when he had soaked up all he could, the map was still a mess.

"Oh, dear!" Two tears squeezed out of Wembley's eyes and raced each other down his nose. "Now what?"

Wembley stood there for a moment, feeling helpless. Then he had an idea. "Wash it! That's what I'll do!" he decided. So he rolled the map up, put it under his arm, and went to see Boober.

Boober loved laundry. So it wasn't surprising that Wembley found him humming over a tub of soap and water.

"Boober! You've got to help me!" Wembley grabbed Boober by his scarf. "I spilled radish shake all over Gobo's map, and I've got to wash it out before he gets back!"

"Washing it . . ." Boober began. But before Boober could say anything more, Wembley had dunked the map right in the tub!

". . . is *not* a good idea." Boober finished what he was trying to say and fished the paper out of the water. "See? It's soaking wet, and the letters are all washed out."

"Oh, *no*," Wembley groaned, covering his eyes. "Now what can I do?"

"First let's hang it on the clothesline to dry," said Boober practically. "Then you should take it to Mokey. She's the best artist in the Rock. Maybe she can draw you another map."

"Great idea!" Wembley cried, feeling a little better. "Thanks, Boober!" He waited and waited until the map was almost dry. Then he rushed out to find Mokey.

Mokey wasn't home. There was a big sign hanging on a stalagmite near her door that read, GONE TO BRUSH-PLANT CAVE. BACK TOMORROW.

Wembley was in despair. "Tomorrow is too late," he said to himself. "I'll have to try to fix Gobo's map myself!"

So he took a handful of Mokey's colored pencils, sat down, and began to trace the outlines of all the caves and tunnels that he could still see on the map. But when he had finished, his drawing didn't look much like a map.

"It'll be all right," Wembley told himself as he rolled the map up again. "It has to be all right!" He rushed back to his cave so that he could replace it before Gobo returned.

When he got there, Wembley tried to unroll the map on Gobo's desk. But it was all wrinkled from being rolled and unrolled while it was still damp.

"It looks like a prune," Wembley worried. "How am I going to flatten it out?"

He tried sitting on it. But that didn't work.

Then he tried putting it under his mattress. But the map only came out looking worse.

Finally Wembley was forced to admit that the map was a mess. It was actually more of a mess now than it had been when he started. It was wrinkled and torn and shredded and . . . and . . . messy. Gobo would never forgive him.

"My best friend won't ever speak to me again," Wembley cried. "He'll never want to see me again! What am I going to do?"

That's when Wembley heard Gobo coming back. He decided what to do in a hurry. He hid under the covers on his bed.

"Wembley?" Gobo called as he entered the cave. Wembley held his breath.

"Guess the little green guy isn't here," Gobo said to himself, heading over to his desk. "I think I'll do some more work on . . ."

Gobo stopped short. "MY MAP!" he yelled. "WHAT HAS HAPPENED TO MY MAP? IT'S RUINED! WEMBLEY?" Gobo turned around and ran out of the cave.

"Well, that does it." Wembley felt as miserable as he had ever felt in his little green life. "Gobo will *never* forgive me. And he certainly won't want to live with me anymore. I guess . . . I'll have to move out."

Wembley started to pack. He put his other banana-tree shirt in a bag. Then he took down the picture Mokey had drawn of him and Gobo.

The picture showed Gobo with his arm around Wembley. Wembley had hung it right by his bed so he could see it every morning when he woke up. Gobo was the bravest and truest Fraggle in Fraggle Rock, and Wembley had been prouder than proud to be his best friend.

"Gobo hates me now," he said sadly to himself. He folded the picture up and put it on top of his shirts.

Wembley was just finishing his packing when Gobo stormed in.

"Wembley!" Gobo yelled, looking very angry indeed. "Where have you been? And what did you do to my map?"

"Oh, Gobo!" Wembley wailed. Then the whole story came tumbling out. "Radish shake . . . washing . . . on the clothesline . . . tried to draw . . . nothing worked . . . hate me!" Wembley pointed to his bag. "Packing . . . move out . . . hate me!" he sobbed.

Gobo took a deep breath. "Wembley, stop crying," he said finally. "I don't hate you."

"You don't?" sniffled Wembley.

"Of course not," Gobo said. "Look, Wembley, sure I'm angry about the map. But I know you didn't do it on purpose."

Wembley shook his head no.

"And I can tell you're very sorry," Gobo went on.

Wembley shook his head yes.

"So I forgive you," Gobo finished.

"You do?" Wembley said in a very little voice.

"I do," Gobo replied. "After all, our friendship is more important than a—than a—piece of paper." Gobo sighed. "Besides, being angry doesn't make you stop caring about someone. It just makes you . . . angry."

"Gee, am I glad to hear that!" Wembley said. "Uh, Gobo? Are you going to yell at me some more now?"

"No, Wembley," Gobo said. "I don't want to yell at you anymore." Then Gobo smiled a little smile.

"I just want to help my best friend unpack!"